This book belongs to:

. . . .

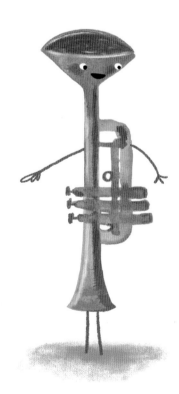

For my two special girls, our hearts will beat together, forever. Love, Dad

Big drum roll and huge thanks to Alan and Susan Windram at LDB
for giving me and this orchestra a chance to play;
and to Catherine Thomann for bringing it all to life - CM

Massive thanks to all the Little Door Books crew, and special thanks
to Vivian French, Edinburgh College of Art friends and my family - CT

Thanks to Colin and Catherine for joining our band.
Special thanks once again to Dave Gray and Paul Croan - LDB

Published by Little Door Books 2018
This edition published 2018
ISBN: 978-0-9927520-7-1
Text copyright © Colin MacIntyre 2018
Illustrations copyright © Catherine Thomann 2018
The right of Colin MacIntyre and Catherine Thomann to be identified as author and illustrator of this
work has been asserted in accordance with the Copyright, Designs and Patents Act 1988.

mail@littledoorbooks.co.uk, www.littledoorbooks.co.uk, twitter: @littledoorbooks

The Humdrum Drum

Colin MacIntyre   Catherine Thomann

One evening as the orchestra was about to play
the most beautiful music, suddenly there was silence.
Drum did not make a sound.

The audience cried 'Ooooo!', then they gasped 'Ahhhh!', and the orchestra conductor was so embarrassed he turned redder than an embarrassed lobster.

In the basement, the concert hall mice stopped ironing immediately. 'Squeak squeak,' they muttered, 'this is not fair, we always iron our finest clothes to the sound of the orchestra playing.'

'What's the matter, Drum?' whispered Harp. 'Why are you not playing with us? We always play together?'

'What's going on?' asked Cymbal.
'The audience are waiting!'

'Drum's feeling humdrum,' sighed Harp. 'He's unhappy because he is always being banged and boomed.'

'But I need you, Drum!' crashed Cymbal. 'What good is a cymbal without the beat of a drum?'

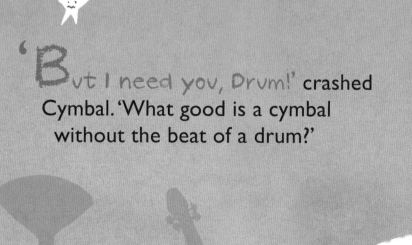

'Hmm,' huffed Drum, now feeling very humdrum. You'll just have to play on without me.'

The next evening, the orchestra was about to make its biggest, most beautiful crescendo, when, once again, everything was quiet. Drum did not make a sound, Cymbal did not crash, and Harp did not pluck...

The audience cried 'Ooooo!', then they gasped 'Ahhhh!', and the orchestra conductor was so embarrassed he turned redder than an embarrassed lobster inside a red post box.

On the roof, the pigeons stopped shaving immediately. 'Coo coo,' they cried, 'this is not fair, we always shave to the sound of the orchestra playing.'

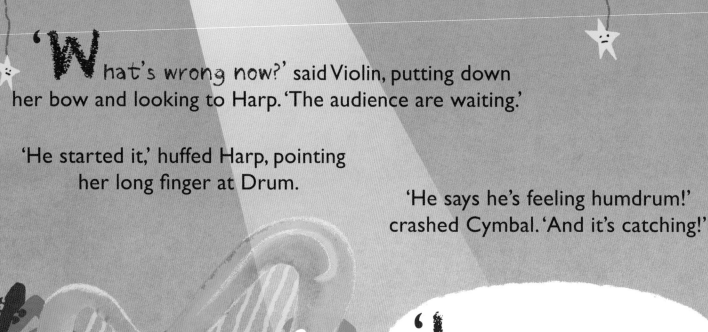

'**W**hat's wrong now?' said Violin, putting down her bow and looking to Harp. 'The audience are waiting.'

'He started it,' huffed Harp, pointing her long finger at Drum.

'He says he's feeling humdrum!' crashed Cymbal. 'And it's catching!'

'**I** don't like being banged and boomed,' moaned Drum. 'It's always the same – bang, bang, bang, boom, boom, boom.'

'And I've had enough of being plucked,' moaned Harp.

'But we need you, Harp, we need you, Drum,' said Violin. 'We have to stick together, without you both we are not a full orchestra.'

'You'll just have to play on without us,' sighed Harp, who was now feeling quite humdrum herself.

The following evening, the orchestra was about to make its biggest, most splendid noise, when, for a third time, not a sound was to be heard. Drum did not boom… Cymbal did not crash… Harp did not pluck… Violin was not bowed… and Trumpet did not toot at all.

The audience cried 'Ooooo!', then they gasped 'Ahhhh!', and the orchestra conductor was so embarrassed he turned redder than an embarrassed lobster inside a red post box covered in crushed tomatoes.

On the balcony the ants stopped washing their dishes immediately. 'This is just not fair,' sighed the ants, 'we always wash up after our evening meal to the sound of the orchestra playing.'

'I stopped because all the others did,' said Violin. 'I don't like the thought of Drum being banged and boomed at all.'

Oh!

Drum started to smile as he listened to the Musical Notes.

'Well,' he began, now feeling a little less humdrum, 'I suppose if you all need me to keep the beat...'

Yay!

'We all need you!' crashed Cymbal.

'I suppose I can pluck again ...' said Harp.

'And we can accompany you all,' agreed Violin and Bow.

'I'm not quite sure why I was feeling humdrum anyway?' tooted Trumpet.

'This will feel much better than being banged and boomed all the time,' beat Drum, now smiling.

At that, Cymbal crashed and the orchestra cheered!

The next evening it was the orchestra's final performance and just as they were about to make their biggest, most rousing sound, there was a pause... then Drum began to beat, Harp plucked, Cymbal crashed, Violin bowed and Trumpet tooted!

And the orchestra conductor was so happy his cheeks beamed redder than an embarrassed lobster inside a red post box covered in crushed tomatoes on the red planet Mars.

SUPER STAR

DRESSING ROOM

SHAVING

Once again, the mice happily ironed, the pigeons shaved, and the ants washed their dishes, all perfectly in time to the orchestra.

The instruments had all played together beautifully as one, to the beat of Drum...

... who wasn't feeling humdrum anymore.

The end

Colin MacIntyre

Colin MacIntyre is an award-winning musician, producer and author, who has written and produced eight albums to date, achieving four top 40 singles and two top 20 albums, most notably under the name Mull Historical Society.

His debut novel, *The Letters of Ivor Punch,* won the 2015 Edinburgh International Book Festival First Book Award.

He has been voted Scotland's Top Creative Talent (Glenfiddich Spirit of Scotland Award) and has toured worldwide, including with The Strokes, Elbow and REM.

Born into a family of writers and storytellers, Colin is a descendant of the Gaelic warrior-poet, Duncan Ban MacIntyre.

He grew up on the isle of Mull in the Hebrides but now lives in London with his family.

For more information about Colin, visit www.colinmacintyre.com and also www.mullhistoricalsociety.com

Catherine Thomann

Catherine Thomann is a Chilean-German graphic designer, artist and author.

Her journey in illustration began on a ship that left Chile travelling to Antarctica. During the voyage she created two illustrated books about the frozen continent.

Her first book, *Niña Alga va a la Antártica,* was published in Santiago de Chile, while her second book, *Antarctic Animals Painting Book,* was published by the United Kingdom Antarctic Heritage Trust in 2010. She has just completed a master's degree in illustration at Edinburgh College of Art.

She enjoys working as a freelance illustrator, as well as creating her own children's books and comics.

For more information on Catherine, visit www. catherinethomann.cl

Look out for our other brilliant picture books.
Visit us at www.littledoorbooks.co.uk

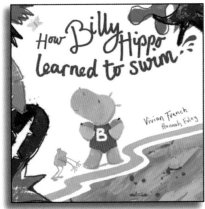

ISBN: 9780992752088

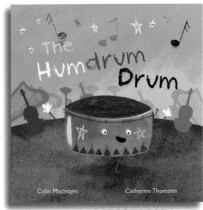

ISBN: 9780992752071

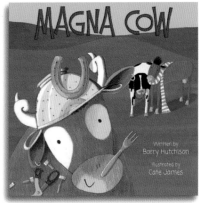

ISBN: 9780992752064

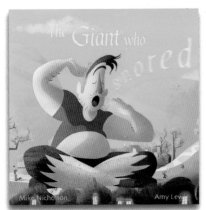

ISBN: 9780992752057

ISBN: 9780992752040

ISBN: 9780992752033

ISBN: 9780992752019

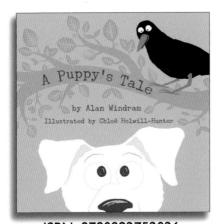

ISBN: 9780992752026

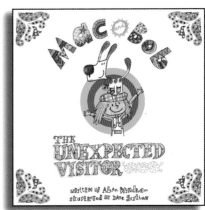

ISBN: 9780992752002